The Riddle of the Drum

The Riddle of the Drum

A Tale from Tizapán, Mexico

Translated and retold by Verna Aardema
illustrated by Tony Chen

Four Winds Press   New York

By the same author

BEHIND THE BACK OF THE MOUNTAIN
TALES FOR THE THIRD EAR
TALES FROM THE STORY HAT
WHY MOSQUITOES BUZZ IN PEOPLE'S EARS
WHO'S IN RABBIT'S HOUSE?
JI-NONGO-NONGO MEANS RIDDLES

Library of Congress Cataloging in Publication Data

Aardema, Verna.
    The riddle of the drum.

    Summary: Anxious to keep his daughter from marrying,
a king announces that no man may marry his daughter
unless he guesses the kind of leather used in a drum made by
a wizard.
    [1. Folklore—Mexico]   I. Chen, Tony.   II. Title.
PZ8.1.A213Ri   398.2'2'0972 [E]   78–23791
ISBN 0–590–07489–X

Published by Four Winds Press
A division of Scholastic Magazines, Inc., New York, N.Y.
Text copyright © 1979 by Verna Aardema
Illustrations copyright © 1979 by Anthony Chen
All rights reserved
Printed in the United States of America
Library of Congress Catalog Card Number: 78–23791
1 2 3 4 5 83 82 81 80 79

For my little Mexicali *sobrina* (niece),
Nadine Gonzalez Aardema,
who lives in Ciudad Victoria, Tamps, Mexico.

There was a king in Tizapán (Tee-sah-PAHN), many years ago, who had a beautiful daughter named Fruela (Froo-AY-lah). He loved her so much, that he decided that whoever married her would have to prove himself worthy.

The king hired a wizard to make a strange drum. The drumhead was from a kind of leather never used before or since. It was black as jet, and the sound it gave forth was like thunder on a distant mountain.

One of the palace guards carried the drum throughout the land, beating upon it and singing:

Tum-te-dum!
The head of the drum-te-dum!
Guess what it's from-te-dum!
And marry the Princess Fruela!

Everywhere he went, the children would fall in line behind him and join the song:

Tum-te-dum!
The head of the drum-te-dum!
Guess what it's from-te-dum!
And marry the Princess Fruela!

Now a handsome prince from a nearby land heard about the riddle of the drum. And he set out to try to win that princess. On the way, he met a man who was running as if a coyote were nipping at his heels.

The prince stopped him and asked why he was going so fast. "I run for fun," said the man. "For I am the runner, Corrín Corrán (Cor-REEN Cor-RAHN)."

"I am Prince Tuzán (Too-SAHN)," said the prince. "I'm on my way to the king, to try to win the princess. If you will help me, I shall reward you."

"I'll do what I can," said Corrín Corrán.
Then on and on went Prince Tuzán —
behind him the runner, Corrín Corrán —
the two marched on toward the palace.

Soon they met a man who carried a bow and a quiver of arrows. The prince greeted him and asked his name.

The man said, "I am the archer, Tirín Tirán (Tee-REEN Tee-RAHN)." Then to show what he could do, he tossed up his sombrero and put an arrow through it in midair!

"Olé (Oh-LAY)!" cried the prince. "Come along and help me win the princess, and I shall reward you."

Then on and on went Prince Tuzán —
behind him the runner, Corrín Corrán;
behind him the archer, Tirín Tirán —
they all marched on toward the palace.

Farther on, they came upon a man who had the largest ears Prince Tuzán had ever seen. He was lying under a tree with one huge ear pressed to the ground.

"Señor (Seh-NYOR), what are you doing?" asked the prince.

The man said, "I am the hearer, Oyín Oyán (Oh-YEEN Oh-YAHN). I am listening to the talk at the palace. Another suitor for the princess has just guessed wrong!"

"Do you know the right answer?" cried the prince, excitedly.

"No," said Oyín Oyán. "But I know all the wrong ones! I know that it isn't:

Duck skin or buck skin,
Goat skin or shoat skin,
Mule skin or mole skin,
Mare skin or bear skin —
Or even armadillo!"

"Come along," said the prince. "If you can keep me from guessing wrong, I shall reward you."

Then on and on went Prince Tuzán —
behind him the runner, Corrín Corrán;
behind him the archer, Tirín Tirán;
behind him the hearer, Oyín Oyán —
they all marched on toward the palace.

They hadn't gone far when they came upon a man who was running a windmill by blowing the fans. With his head tilted back and his cheeks puffed out, he BLEW—and the windmill turned!

"How extraordinary!" cried the prince.

"Quite ordinary for me," explained the man. "For I am the blower, Soplín Soplán (So-PLEEN So-PLAHN)."

"Come along," said the prince. "Help me win the princess, and I shall reward you."

Then on and on went Prince Tuzán —
behind him the runner, Corrín Corrán;
behind him the archer, Tirín Tirán;
behind him the hearer, Oyín Oyán —
behind him the blower, Soplín Soplán —
they all marched on toward the palace.

They were all becoming tired and hungry, when they came upon a man who was roasting a whole ox over a fire pit.

The prince asked, "Señor, are you cooking all this meat for yourself?"

"Sí (See)," said the man. "I am the eater, Comín Comán (Co-MEEN Co-MAHN). For me, this is just one BIG meatball!" But he invited them to share the meat.

They ate, and waited for the eater to finish the rest so that he could join them.

Then on and on went Prince Tuzán —
behind him the runner, Corrín Corrán;
behind him the archer, Tirín Tirán;
behind him the hearer, Oyín Oyán;
behind him the blower, Soplín Soplán;
behind him the eater, Comín Comán —
they all marched on toward the palace.

Soon they rounded the crest of a hill and saw the palace of the king gleaming on the far hillside.

Now it happened that the princess was on her balcony. Oyín Oyán put an ear to the ground and heard her say, "Papá, a prince is coming."

The king appeared on the balcony. And the hearer heard him say, "Sí! And he has uno, dos, tres, cuatro, cinco (OO-no, dose, trase, QUAH-tro, SEEN-ko) attendants! Too bad he has to die — just because he doesn't know that the drumhead is made from the skin of a . . . " And he *said* the word!

Oyín Oyán leaped up so fast, his ears flapped! "I know the answer to the riddle!" he cried. Then he whispered it to the prince.

When Prince Tuzán and his men reached the palace, they were taken at once into the presence of the king.

The prince bowed and said, "Your Majesty, I have come to solve the riddle of the drum."

"Are you aware," said the king, "that if you fail, you forfeit your life?"

"Sí," said the prince. "Show me the drum."

The guard came in beating the drum and singing:

Tum-te-dum!
The head of the drum-te-dum!
Guess what it's from-te-dum!
And marry the Princess Fruela!

Prince Tuzán ran his fingers over the thin black skin of the drumhead. He tapped out a little rhythm, saying as he tapped: "It isn't

Duck skin or buckskin,
Goat skin or shoat skin,
Mule skin or mole skin,
Mare skin or . . . "

"Don't tell me what it isn't!" bellowed the king. "Tell me what it IS!"

Prince Tuzán said, "It appears to me that this is the skin of a very LARGE flea!"

"!Uf (Oof)!" snorted the king. He shook his head in amazement! But he had to admit that Prince Tuzán was right! Then he said, "But there are two more things you must do before you may marry my daughter! First, one of your servants and one of my servants will race to the sea and fetch water. If mine returns first, you lose your life!"

Corrín Corrán stepped forward. "Prince Tuzán, allow me to run for you," he said. Of course the prince was happy to let him.

Corrín Corrán laughed when he saw who was running for the king. It was a wrinkled old woman in a long gray dress, with a black rebozo around her shoulders.

But after they began to run, he realized that the woman was a witch! He had to run with all his might just to keep even with her!

Side-by-side they raced down the valley, past a jacaranda tree, then over a little hill, and out upon the beach. At the sea, they filled their small bottles and turned back at the same moment.

Now, Corrín Corrán knew he *had* to win, to save the life of the prince! He sprinted, and reached the tree three meters ahead of the woman.

Then she screamed, "SLEEP!"

Corrín Corrán collapsed upon the path and was instantly asleep and snoring!

Oyín Oyán heard the witch. He saw Corrín Corrán fall! He cried, "Tirín Tirán, shoot the tree!"

The archer let an arrow fly. ZAP! It went into the tree trunk above the sleeping runner. Corrín Corrán woke up and leaped back into the race.

But the old woman was far ahead.

Soplín Soplán saw her coming straight for the finish line. He puffed out his cheeks and aimed a strong wind at her!

The old woman's skirt fluttered!Her rebozo blew off! Then the wind lifted her up and carried her — kicking and screeching — all the way back to the jacaranda tree!

Of course, Corrín Corrán finished first.

"You cheated!" protested the king. But he knew that the witch had not played fair, either. So he said no more about it. Anyway, he was confident he would stop the prince with the next task.

He said, "Before sundown, one of your servants must eat a cartload of food! If he fails, you will die!"

A cart heaped with tacos, tortillas (tor-TEE-yahs), meatballs, and puddings was brought in. Comín Comán set to! Before evening, he had eaten everything — even the cart!

When the king saw that the tasks were accomplished, he gave Prince Tuzán the Princess Fruela in marriage. The two lived together happily for many years.

And the runner, Corrín Corrán; the archer, Tirín Tirán; the hearer, Oyín Oyán; the blower, Soplín Soplán; and the eater, Comín Comán all lived with them at the palace.

Bibliography

The Riddle of the Drum, A Tale from Tizapán, Mexico is translated and retold from "El Aro de Hinojo y El Cuero de Piojo" in *Tales from Jalisco, Mexico,* by Howard T. Wheeler, published by the American Folk-lore Society, printed at the Rydal Press, Sante Fe, New Mexico, 1943.

Glossary

Corrín Corrán: From the Spanish verb *correr*, meaning *to run*

Tirín Tirán: From *tirar, to shoot*

Olé: Great

Soplín Soplán: From *soplar, to blow*

Señor: Mister

Oyín Oyán: From *oir, to hear*

Sí: Yes

Comín Comán: From *comer, to eat*

Uno, dos, tres, cuatro, cinco: One, two, three, four, five

Uf: Ugh

Rebozo (Ray-BOH-soh): Scarf

Jacaranda (Hah-cah-RAHN-dah): A tropical tree having purplish blue
     flowers

Zap (Sahp): Bam